To my best friend and husband,
and to many more moons together
—H. K.

To Marjorie Powell,
who taught me about the gibbous moon
—J. P.

Book design by Katie Jennings.
Typeset in Sonopa and Simran.
The illustrations in this book were rendered in gouache and permanent masking medium on paper.
Manufactured in China.

Library of Congress Cataloging-in-Publication Data

Khan, Hena.
Night of the Moon : a Muslim holiday story / by Hena Khan : illustrated by Julie Paschkis.
p. cm.
Summary: Yasmeen has a wonderful time celebrating the Muslim holy month
of Ramadan with her family and friends.
ISBN 978-0-8118-6062-8
[1. Ramadan—Fiction. 2. Muslims—fiction. 3. Islam—Customs and practices—Fiction.
4. Fasts and feasts—Islam—Fiction.] I. Paschkis, Julie, ill. II. Title
PZ7.K52652NIG 2008
[E]—dc22
2007024962

10 9 8 7 6 5 4 3 2

Chronicle Books LLC
680 Second Street, San Francisco, California 94107

www.chroniclekids.com

NIGHT of the MOON

By Hena Khan

Illustrated by Julie Paschkis

chronicle books · san francisco

It was bedtime, and Yasmeen waited for her mom to read her a story as she did every night. But this night was different.

Mom came into her room and pulled back the curtains that hung over the window. "Come and take a look at the moon," she said.

"What's so special about the moon?" Yasmeen wondered.

"See for yourself," Mom said.

"That tiny little line?" Yasmeen asked as she squinted into the darkness. "I can hardly see it."

"That's because it's the moon's first crescent," Mom said. "It means a new month is beginning."

"A new month?" Yasmeen asked. "But it's only the seventeenth."

"It's a new month in the **Islamic** calendar, which is based on the moon," Mom explained. "Long ago, people used the shape of the moon to keep track of days. They'd watch the moon grow bigger till it was full, then smaller till it disappeared. When the moon reappeared, a new month would begin."

"Like tonight," Yasmeen said.

"Exactly. And do you know what month is starting tonight?" Mom asked.

"The month of Ramadan!" Yasmeen answered.

Yasmeen had been looking forward to **ramadan**.
It was a time filled with delicious foods, new clothes,
lots of parties, and her favorite thing ever—presents!

At school the next day, Yasmeen was proud when
her class had a discussion about Ramadan.

Her teacher, Mr. Sanchez, told the class, "During the month of Ramadan, many Muslim people **fast** each day. Does anyone know what that means?"

Yasmeen did! "It means you don't eat or drink anything all day long," she shared. "You wake up before sunrise to eat, and then you don't have anything else until the sun goes down."

Everyone had lots of questions about fasting. They especially wanted to know if kids had to do it.

"Little kids don't fast," Yasmeen said. "But maybe I'll try it for a day next year."

Yasmeen imagined a day without lunch. Or snacks. Or even a drink of water!

That afternoon, while Yasmeen and her little brother, Bilal, had snacks at home, Yasmeen asked her mom if fasting was hard.

"It can be hard sometimes, but I don't mind," Mom answered. "Fasting helps me remember to be grateful for the food I have and to be more patient."

As the sun slowly started to go down in the sky, Yasmeen helped Mom pile a plate high with fresh dates and prepare a pitcher of milk. These were the traditional foods to eat after the fast.

Finally, sunset came, and Dad passed around the dates and said a little prayer. Everyone bit into the sweet, chewy fruits together, and the first fast of Ramadan was over. Then it was time for a special dinner with everyone's favorite foods.

That weekend Yasmeen's family went to her cousin Humza's house for the first of many Ramadan parties. Her aunt and uncle served a big dinner of beef kabobs, grilled vegetables, and fresh bread. Then there were tons of desserts—everything from chocolate fudge cake to rice pudding.

After dinner, Yasmeen peeked out the window at the moon. It looked like it was stuffed with good food, too, since it was now a thick crescent.

The next week, Mom and Dad spent hours in the kitchen cooking up huge pots of food to bring to the mosque. Yasmeen and Bilal made cupcakes, too.

"Ramadan is a time for sharing," Dad explained. "Not everyone has as much to eat as we do."

The mosque was filled with people that weekend, and soon, all of the cupcakes were gone. As Yasmeen walked outside after evening prayers she felt good about helping others. She looked up at the moon, which was half full now—like a half-eaten cupcake.

The days of Ramadan quickly flew by. Every night, Yasmeen looked for the moon.

One night, when Grandma was visiting, she and Yasmeen went for a walk after dinner. Together, they saw that the moon was a brilliant circle.

"It's so pretty," said Yasmeen, wishing she could see it closer.

"subhanallah," said Grandma.

That was what Grandma said whenever she saw something wonderful. It was her way of being thankful for beautiful things.

The full moon meant that Ramadan was
already half over. Yasmeen couldn't believe it.

The next weekend it was time for Yasmeen's family to have a Ramadan party. Lots of friends and family came over in the evening for a big backyard barbecue. Dad set up a trampoline in the yard, and Yasmeen, Bilal, and Humza took turns leaping toward the stars, pretending they were on the moon.

Meanwhile, a real half moon shone in the sky.

Over the next week, Yasmeen watched as the moon slowly changed to a crescent and then to a thin line. The month of Ramadan was coming to an end.

Finally, one night the sky was moonless. As hard as she looked into the blackness outside her window, Yasmeen couldn't find the moon at all.

"There's no more moon!" Yasmeen announced to her family.

Yasmeen couldn't wait for tomorrow, when the moon's first crescent would appear for a very special night: **the night of the moon.**

The Night of the Moon meant that Ramadan was over, and the following day would be the holiday of ɛid.

When the sun set the next evening, Yasmeen's family went to the community center for a Night of the Moon celebration. Decorated with lights and shiny balloons, the place looked magical. There were lots of stalls where people sold clothes, jewelry, toys, snacks, and gifts

from different countries. Yasmeen bought some green metal bangles from India that jingled on her wrist. Bilal got a red hat with a big tassel that came from Turkey. And Mom picked out new clothes for the family to wear on Eid, including a pretty green dress for Yasmeen!

Later that night, Yasmeen had her hands painted with henna paste, in a beautiful pattern with moons and stars. The paste left a dark orange dye on her palms that would last for about a week, and then fade away. Yasmeen was excited to show her friends at school.

When the family got home that night, Yasmeen caught a glimpse of the moon's first crescent, so thin it was like a faint line of chalk in the sky.

The next morning, Yasmeen woke up to the sound of Bilal shouting, **"eid mubarak!"** This was the traditional greeting of Eid, a very happy day for Muslims all over the world.

After a big breakfast together, Yasmeen and her family dressed up in their new clothes and went to the mosque for Eid prayers. Everyone gathered on the lawn to wish each other a happy holiday and exchange the three hugs of Eid.

Then Yasmeen's family visited friends and relatives for the rest of the day. Everywhere they went, Yasmeen and Bilal received little gifts of money called *eidee*.

For Yasmeen, though, the best part of the holiday—
better than the henna, the new dress, and all the
Eidee money she collected—was the surprise she got
at bedtime.

Mom and Dad called her into the family room and
handed her a big box wrapped in shiny silver paper.

"It's an Eid present, Yasmeen," Mom said, smiling. "To
help you watch for Ramadan to come again next year."

Yasmeen tore the paper off the box. It was a huge telescope! She stayed up late with Dad putting it together and setting it up in her bedroom. Then she took a look at the sky from the window, and this is what she saw . . .

"subhanallah," Yasmeen whispered as she looked at the wonderful moon. She couldn't wait for Ramadan next year.

author's notes

The moon is an important symbol for Muslims around the world because the Islamic calendar is based on the lunar cycle. There are twelve months in the Islamic calendar, the ninth of which is Ramadan—the month during which the Muslim holy book, the Quran, was first received by Prophet Muhammad over 1,400 years ago. Ramadan traditionally begins and ends with the sighting of the moon's first crescent.

During Ramadan, the holiest month of the year, healthy adult Muslims are expected to fast from sunrise to sunset daily. Reasons for fasting include remembering God and self-discipline. Muslims are also encouraged to give to charity, perform good deeds, and offer special prayers during the month.

The Night of the Moon celebration, or *Chaand Raat* in the Urdu language (spoken in Pakistan and India), is a popular cultural tradition from South Asia. In the United States, Muslims from different backgrounds often join together on the last night of Ramadan to celebrate its successful completion and to prepare for the Eid holiday—a religious festival the next day.

---

glossary

Eid (EED): an Islamic festival. Eid-ul-Fitr is the full name of the festival that falls on the day after Ramadan ends.

Eidee (EED-ee): a traditional gift of money given to children on Eid.

henna: a dye made from dried leaves used to decorate skin with a dark orange tint that fades away over a couple of weeks.

Islam: a religion based on the Quran and the teaching of Prophet Muhammad.

mosque (mosk): a place where Muslims gather to pray together.

mubarak (moo-BAR-uk): roughly translates to "blessed" from Arabic. *Eid Mubarak*, a phrase that means "may you enjoy a blessed festival," is used as a greeting on the holiday.

muslim: a person who practices the religion of Islam.

Quran (koor-RAHN): the holy book of Muslims.

ramadan (RAHM-uh-dahn): the ninth month in the Islamic calendar, and the holiest month for Muslims.

subhanallah (soob-HAHN-ul-LAH): roughly translates to "Glory to God" from Arabic.